CW00868239
Just Me
and
My fish
J. Robert Lindesmith

This is a work of fiction. Names, characters, places and incidents either are the product of the author's imagination or are used fictitiously, and any resemblance to any actual persons, living or dead, events, or locales is entirely coincidental.

To order additional copies of this book, contact:
Xlibris
1-888-795-4274
www.Xlibris.com
Orders@Xlibris.com

Illustrated by Dwight Nacaytuna

ISBN: Softcover 978-1-7960-6831-3
Hardcover 978-1-7960-6832-0
EBook 978-1-7960-6830-6

Print information available on the last page

Rev. date: 10/29/2019

Just Me and My fish

There comes times

Where you can't find

A friend.

So I sit and look.

Tried a book.

Tired to social.

But to my fail.

My eyes brought me back upon your sail.

And there was just me and my fish.

A smile everyone should have.

My lips drawing up.

A meaningful day for which you should become.

Like you...

Me and my fish.

The beauty upon your free forming
quest every day Helped me rest.

Into a mind casting zest.

Of life.

Of once was and has changed upon
those that cast a line upon my being.

My appearance.

My talk.

My walk.

But I'm Me.

Just me...

Is it a world that will bring me
upon capture or let me go?

To become what mysterious events might show ?

Those that question my color?

You swimming in blue skin

I didn't question that look.

Just marvel in it day and before I rest.

I dislike that they "bully" upon me.

But within my strength I grow to
understand their insecurity .

Never questioned your gender.

For who we are gives to nothing.

And no one.

Firing off peace, love and caring for each other.

And those to come.

I thought of Good Night Moon.

A breakfast with green eggs and ham.

Memories raising what was and where I am.

F

Just one fish teaching me everyday
that tomorrow is a new day.

For those with anger and deception.

Feed me with your wrong words
and wrong direction AND I will keep
swimming right where I want to go.

For I Matter.

If you care for me

I will bring you joy.

So stop.

And look what you and I can become.

Because You Matter too.

I'm stronger than you because

Courage is in my belief.

My crayon box

Doesn't make a difference .

It makes us better and the same within the pack.

So I watched a fish within glass walls flow
within our world and took a deep breath.

Living without fear, just me and my fish.

YOU
MATTER.

CPSIA information can be obtained
at www.ICGtesting.com
Printed in the USA
BVHW021012071119
563172BV00002B/8/P